BOOK ONE

Missing Monkey!

OTHER CHAPTER BOOKS BY MARY AMATO

BOOK ONE

GOOD CROOKS

Missing Monkey!

Mary Amato

Illustrated by **Ward Jenkins**

EGMONT

NEW YORK • USA

EGMONT

We bring stories to life

First published by Egmont USA, 2014
443 Park Avenue South, Suite 806
New York, NY 10016

Text copyright © Mary Amato, 2014
Illustrations copyright © Ward Jenkins, 2014
All rights reserved

1 3 5 7 9 8 6 4 2

www.egmontusa.com
www.maryamato.com
www.wardjenkins.com

Library of Congress Cataloging-in-Publication Data
Amato, Mary.
Missing monkey! / by Mary Amato ; illustrated by Ward Jenkins.
pages cm. -- (Good crooks ; book 1)
Summary: Tired of being pressured to help commit crimes and
yearning for a more normal life, twins Jillian and Billy band
together to do good deeds while their parents kidnap a monkey
from the zoo, hoping to teach it to steal. Includes activities.
ISBN 978-1-60684-396-3 (hardcover) -- ISBN 978-1-60684-509-7
(digest pbk.) [1. Conduct of life--Fiction. 2. Robbers and outlaws--
Fiction. 3. Brothers and sisters--Fiction. 4. Twins--Fiction.
5. Family life--Fiction.] I. Jenkins, Ward, illustrator. II. Title.
PZ7.A49165Mis 2014
[Fic]--dc23   2013018251
ISBN 978-1-60684-403-8 (eBook)

Printed in the United States of America

Contents

1

The Cops Are Coming

"This is it," my dad said. "The back door to the Chicago Bank."

"The cops are going to be here any second," my sister added.

The three of us were dressed in black turtlenecks and our sneaky black caps.

You guessed it. My dad is a robber. So is my mom. Ron and Tanya Crook. They want my sister, Jillian, and me to follow in their footsteps.

Dad handed me a sharp metal tool. "Slide it into the lock and jiggle it until the lock pops open."

I slid the metal pick in and jiggled it. My face started to sweat.

"You look scared," Jillian whispered.

I was going to say, "You look like a baboon," but that's the problem with having a twin. If I tell her she's ugly, I'm not doing myself any favor. We both have the same freckles, the same big ears, the same knobby knees, and the same giant feet.

The only thing that's different about Jillian and me is our pigtails.

2

She has two and I have three. Just kidding, I buzzed my pigtails off last year and gave them to pigs without tails. Just kidding, I've been pigtail-free all my life.

"Focus, Billy. Think of all that money we're going to steal," Dad whispered.

I pictured us running out with bags of cash, and then I pictured the bank owners coming in to find an

empty safe. They would be so sad.

WHAT?????? I'm a Crook. Crooks shouldn't think about how sad the bank owners will be!

I glanced at my dad. He was bouncing on his toes. His ten little piggies were happy just thinking about money.

A thought dropped out of my brain: *I do not want to rob any more banks. I want to do something nice for a change!*

I dropped the pick. What was happening to me?

Suddenly the door opened and a beam of light hit us.

A tall guard lunged at me. I ducked, and the guard grabbed my dad. "Got you!"

"This is it," Dad cried. "The end of our Crook ways!"

"Good going, bro," Jillian said.

The guard laughed and turned on the lights. He wasn't really a guard. He was my mom. We weren't really at the back door of the Chicago Bank. We were at home, taking a test on lock picking. And the "bank door" was our closet.

Mom took off her hat and fluffed up her spiky black hair. "Billy, did you practice?"

I didn't have to say a word. My bright red face did all the talking.

"No bacon on your burger tonight," she said.

"Yeah," Dad said. "Jillian, you take a turn. Then we'll make Billy do it over till he gets it right."

I held out the pick to my sister.

"Keep it," Jillian said. "I invented a new lock opener." She pulled a small black gadget from her pocket. "I call it the Popper."

"That's the remote control for your TV," I said.

She grinned. "I reprogrammed it."

"Cool!" Dad said. "That's what you've been working on all week?"

"Enough with the chatter." Mom was ready to get cracking. "Places! You've got exactly sixty seconds to unlock the door, Jillian."

"No problem!" Jillian said, turning off the lights.

Mom locked herself in the closet and yelled, "Go!"

Jillian pointed her gadget at the door and hit a button.

Pop!

She turned the knob and the door opened.

My parents went mad crazy.

Mom hugged her.

"Woohoo!" Dad exclaimed. "Does it work on any lock?"

"I think so," Jillian said.

"Fantastic!" Mom flipped on the lights. "Can you make more of those?"

Jillian shrugged. "Sure. I can make one for each of us."

Mom turned to me. "Billy, do you know what this means?"

"It's going to be hard to switch TV channels?" I guessed.

"No! With Jillian's new gadget, *you'll* be a successful crook, too!" Mom took the Popper out of Jillian's hand and put it in mine.

"Cash! Jewels! Gold!" Dad started dancing around.

I danced around to make my parents think I was happy. Deep inside I wasn't sure I wanted to be a crook anymore. *That* was a big problem.

2

Don't Forget Your Purse

The next morning, a golden beam of sunlight shot through my window and punched me right in the face. I looked at the clock by my bed: 8:00 A.M.

Mom and Dad would want me to snooze all morning and spend the afternoon stealing, but I couldn't get back to sleep.

I put on my stockings, a polka-dotted dress, and a pair of granny kicks.

You guessed it. My old-lady
costume. Jillian and I always have to
wear a disguise if we leave the house.
All Crooks do.

I topped off my outfit with a curly
gray wig and glasses. One of my best
costumes. I call her Mrs. Whiffbacon.
Why? I love the whiff of bacon, of
course.

Last but not least, I grabbed my
big brown purse. By the way, big

brown purses are very handy. You can
stuff a lot of junk into a purse: a wig,
a ninja grappling hook, wet wipes to
get rid of fingerprints. After you've
carried a purse for a while, you just
feel naked without it.

In the kitchen, Jillian was typing
away on her laptop. She was up this
early every morning.

"Hey, Billy," she said.

"Working on your next crime tool?" I asked.

"Maybe." She turned her laptop so I couldn't see.

I grabbed a bag of cookies for breakfast. While I ate them, I glanced out the window. It was a sunny Saturday. The boy who lived across the street was mowing our neighbor's lawn. Old Mr. Nelson hobbled out and tried to pay him, but the boy waved away the money.

What a nice *boy*, I thought. I'd like to help an old person. And then I choked on my cookie. Crooks shouldn't want to do good deeds!

"What's wrong with you?" Jillian asked. "Forget how to swallow?"

I got up quickly and headed toward our back door.

"Where you going?" Jillian called.

I had to get some fresh air, and some bacon to go with it. I cut through the backyard and headed downtown. We move around a lot and had only been in Lincoln Park a few weeks, so I was still getting to know the neighborhood.

I stopped at the jewelry store on the corner. The store wasn't open until ten. Down the street, a man was heading into Mither's Restaurant— excellent bacon-and-grilled-cheese sandwiches, by the way. Otherwise the block was quiet. This was a perfect time to be a real crook. Imagine how proud Ron and Tanya Crook would be if I stole a diamond ring before they even got out of bed.

I slipped Jillian's lock opener out of my purse. I pointed it at the door and was about to press the button when a poster taped in the window caught my eye. The world's biggest case of goose bumps prickled every inch of my skin.

CLEANUP DAY
AT THE ZOO

VOLUNTEERS
ENTER
HERE ➡

You will always succeed if you do a good deed.

A movie began to play in my mind, starring me, Billy Crook. In the movie, I was weeding the flowers next to the Monkey House at the zoo. I was smiling. The zookeepers were smiling. Even the baboons were smiling.

Just imagining it made me feel all warm inside, like the sun was shining on my great big beating heart.

Wait! I thought. *I should be dreaming of crimes, not good deeds!*

My hand began to shake. I looked in the jewelry store window. Diamond rings. Ruby necklaces. Pearl bracelets. That loot could be mine. But I put the lock opener back in my purse, turned away, and began to race down the street.

A car drove by, and a teenager

stuck his head out the window. "Go, Grandma!"

Ooops. I slowed to turtle speed.

I passed by Mither's, the smell of bacon drifting out the door, but kept walking. After a few blocks, I stopped and pretended to rest on a city bench. I pulled a mirror out of my purse to put on fresh lipstick. Actually, my lips looked fine. I was just using the mirror to see if I was being followed.

The coast looked clear. I began walking again. Just ahead, I could see the green-and-blue flag of the zoo. Was I really going to do a good deed?

Was I really going to pass up the chance to steal? Was I really going to pass up the chance to eat bacon? Was I out of my mind?

3

Watch Out for Grandma

"**W**elcome! Thank you so much for coming! Are you ready to do some gardening?" A round-cheeked woman in a zoo uniform handed me a pair of gardening gloves. Her name tag read SALLY MANDER, ZOO DIRECTOR.

People were streaming into the zoo entrance. Moms, dads, kids, and even old grandmas like me had all come to work. The birds were singing. The sun was shining. Goodness seemed to be springing up from the ground.

"We need grass mowing, tree trimming, and garden weeding," Ms. Mander said. "Where would you like to work?"

I looked around. "How about by the monkeys?"

She took me over to the Monkey House. Inside the big cage, the monkeys were climbing on trees and playing on tire swings. A small monkey jumped onto a platform loaded with bananas near the front of the cage.

"Hi, Razzle," the director said. "How's my boy today?"

"Eh oooh," Razzle said.

Another monkey joined Razzle next to the bananas on the platform.

"Here's your sister!" The director clapped her hands. "Hi, Dazzle!"

Razzle and Dazzle clapped their hands, too.

"This nice woman is going to make your area beautiful!" Ms. Mander pointed at me.

I waved at Razzle and Dazzle. They waved back. I think they liked me.

All around the area, the flower beds were choked with ugly weeds. The monkeys watched as Ms. Mander showed how to pull the weeds so the flowers could grow.

Okay. Time to get to work.

Yank! Yoink! Yank!

Zoink! Zink! Zoink!

I didn't just yank out the weeds. I defeated them. *Say good-bye, weeds! You have finally met your match! That's how I roll.*

An old woman wearing a big floppy hat walked up. "Looks much better."

"Ooohh eeeh eehheh," Razzle and Dazzle exclaimed.

I trimmed the dead leaves off the flowers, and the old woman handed me a watering can to give them a drink.

"Nice job." The old woman clapped.

Razzle and Dazzle clapped, too, and I had to laugh.

It feels good to do a good deed, I thought. Then I dropped the watering can in shock.

I was doing a good deed and enjoying it! All my life I had been taught that doing good was bad. But if doing good made me feel good, then how could it be bad?

"Is this your first time here, Mrs. Whiffbacon?" the old woman asked.

I almost croaked. How could she know my name? She lifted her floppy hat and glasses. It wasn't an old woman. It was my sister, wearing her Mrs. Sippy costume. I should've recognized the plain blue dress. I've worn that dress!

"Jillian!" I exclaimed.

"Shh," she whispered. Then she said in her best Mrs. Sippy accent,

"Come along, Mrs. Whiffbacon. I want to show you something over here." She pulled me to the side of the Monkey House. Our monkey friends scampered after us as if they wanted to listen.

"Billy," she whispered, "you were acting weird last night and this morning. So I followed you. What are you doing here?"

"I'm—I came here because . . ." I stopped. I took a big breath. "Jillian, I want to do something nice for a change."

The truth popped out of me!

I felt better, lighter, like somebody had

weeded and watered me. But I had a big problem. Jillian was going to freak out. She'd probably tell my parents the whole story.

Behind her glasses, my sister's eyes were huge. "I can't believe you just said that."

"I know." I sighed. "I'm nuts."

"No! That's not what I mean, Billy. I mean, I . . . I feel the same way," she said.

I was shocked. "You're kidding? You want to do something good, too?"

She nodded.

"But what about all your crime inventions?"

"Ever since I was six and invented that fingerprint eraser, Mom and Dad want me to keep inventing more stuff to help them steal. So that's what I've been doing. But lately . . ." She leaned closer. "You know Mr. Nelson?"

"The old guy who lives next to us?"

She nodded. "I noticed that he has trouble unlocking his door because his hands are so old. So I invented the lock opener and I put one in his mailbox. For free."

"That's so nice!" I said.

She frowned. "I know. Mom and Dad would be horrified."

I wasn't alone. My sister wanted to do good deeds, too! Joy bubbled up from somewhere deep inside my soul. "Woohoo!" I yelled, and began jumping.

"Ooohoo!" The monkeys went

crazy, yelling and jumping, too.

"Whoa, Grandma," Jillian said. "Remember where we are."

I stopped and straightened my dress and wig.

Just then we heard a familiar voice. "Good morning, ladies!"

We turned to see two construction workers walking toward us.

"Oh, no," Jillian whispered. "It's Mom and Dad!"

4

Ee–ee Uh-oh

Mom and Dad strolled up in their favorite disguises. They were wearing orange vests and hard hats. Their boots were dirty, as if they'd been working all day. Mom had a full beard. Dad had a bushy mustache.

Were Mom and Dad spying on us? Did they know we were here at the zoo to do a good deed?

I looked at Jillian. She was playing it cool. "Good morning," she said in her Mrs. Sippy voice.

Dad was carrying orange cones, which he began to set out. Mom had a clipboard and was pretending to write down stuff.

"So . . . ," Dad whispered, "what's shaking?"

"Not much," Jillian whispered back. "What are you doing here?"

"When we woke up and found both of you gone so early," Mom explained, "we got worried."

"But how did you find us?" I asked.

"We have our ways, Billy." She smiled. "Why on earth did you come to the zoo?"

"We—we—" Jillian's mind must have gone blank. It didn't happen

often. She looked at me for help.

"We—we—" My mind had gone blank, too.

"Ee—ee—!" Razzle and Dazzle said, copying us.

"Check it out!" I laughed, and pointed at the monkeys, trying to change the subject. "Those monkeys do everything we do!"

Mom and Dad turned to look at the hairy little guys.

"I get it!" Mom said.

My knees started to shake.

"You do?" Jillian's voice quivered.

"You're both brilliant!" Mom said.

"We are?" I was so confused.

"Yes!" Mom exclaimed. "You came here to kidnap a monkey! To take it home and teach it to steal!"

Dad patted me on the back. "That is brilliant! Let's do it!"

Steal a monkey! Were they serious?

Dad started bouncing. "Jillian, do you have your lock opener?"

"Billy had it last," Mom said. "Did you bring it?" Before I could stop her, she grabbed my purse and found the lock opener under my candy bar. "Ron, create a distraction. I'll steal the monkey."

"Wait!" I said.

But Ron and Tanya Crook don't wait. Mom slipped through a back gate marked KEEP OUT. Dad marched over to Sally Mander.

"Ma'am, please clear the area around the Monkey House for a few minutes while I fix the walkway," Dad said. "I need to keep everyone safe."

"Certainly!" Sally Mander said, leading Mrs. Sippy and me away.

A few seconds later, Jillian got a text on her cell phone from Dad to meet at the corner of Lincoln and Webster.

"Maybe the lock opener didn't

work," Jillian whispered. "And Mom didn't steal a monkey."

"Yeah," I said. But we both knew that was a long shot. Jillian is a genius. Her gadgets always work.

We speed-walked as fast as our granny legs could go. Our parents were waiting in our white van . . . and they didn't look happy. Maybe the famous Crooks hadn't gotten the monkey after all!

We got in, and Dad drove off.

"Your lock popper didn't work, Jillian," Mom said.

Jillian and I traded a secret happy smile.

Then Mom lifted up a sack. "Just kidding! Meet the newest member of the Crook family!"

Razzle hopped out.

"Eeeeh ee e?" he screeched, and scratched his head. Then he started going bananas.

Yep. That's what really happened. When most families go to the zoo, they come home with happy memories. When the Crook family goes, we come home with a wild animal.

5

Monkey Breath

After a few minutes of oo ooing and ee eeing, Razzle the monkey calmed down. He hopped on Mom's shoulder and looked over the front seat at Jillian and me.

"Eeeeh ee e?" he asked.

It's as if he was asking us to fix his problem.

"Mom," I said, "maybe we should take the monkey back."

She laughed. "Why?"

"How can we hide a monkey? The cops will find him," I said.

"We're good at hiding things, Billy," Dad said. "We've kept you hi—"

Mom jumped in. "We'll get him a disguise."

"But he has a sister named Dazzle," Jillian added. "They'll miss each other."

Mom gave her a strange look. "Since when do we care about stuff like that? He'll love living with us!"

"Oooh ooh eeeh!" Dad started making monkey noises, and Razzle looked at him like he was nuts.

Jillian took off her glasses and wig, and her pigtails popped out.

Razzle's round black eyes almost jumped out of his small face. "Hoo eeh ooo?" He rubbed his face and scratched his head. Then he hopped onto Jillian's lap and pulled her hair.

"Ouch!" Jillian said.

"Ooch!" Razzle screeched.

"Hey, be nice!" I said, pulling off my glasses and wig.

The monkey jumped on my shoulder and stuck his finger up my right nostril.

"Yuck!" I pushed his hairy arm away.

He leaned over and breathed in my face. If you've never smelled monkey breath, you're lucky. This guy's breath could kill a cow.

"Mom," I said, "this monkey is a maniac! You have to take him back."

"No way, Billy. We're just getting started," Mom said. "Ron, pull into that shopping mall parking lot."

Jillian and I traded glances.

Dad pulled into the lot.

"I'm going to get a disguise for the monkey." Mom took a handful of fake one-hundred-dollar bills from the glove compartment, fixed her beard in the mirror, and got out. "I'll hurry. Keep the monkey happy!"

Mom was gone exactly eleven minutes. And if you think eleven minutes is short, try spending it in a locked car with a mad crazy monkey.

Here's what a monkey will do in eleven minutes:

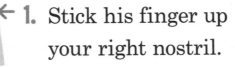

1. Stick his finger up your right nostril.
2. Lick your eyebrow.
3. Jump on your head.
4. Jump on your sister's head.
5. Throw your dad's hat out the window.
6. Make your dad's bald head even shinier by licking it seven times.

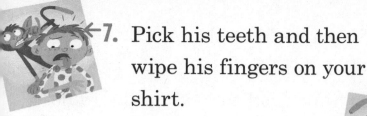

7. Pick his teeth and then wipe his fingers on your shirt.
8. Sing along with the → radio. Very badly. In your ear.
9. Sneeze. In your face. Twice.
10. Repeat all of the above.

Dad thought it was hilarious.

Mom finally came back, pushing a baby stroller with a big bag on top of it. She grabbed the bag and hopped in. "Every Crook needs a costume." She dressed the monkey in pink baby pajamas and tied on a pink baby bonnet. "Baby Razzle Crook. Isn't she cute?"

"It's a he," I said.

"Ee!" said Razzle.

"Shhh." Dad turned up the radio. "Listen."

The news was on. "Breaking news: a monkey is missing from the zoo. While hundreds of volunteers were starting to fix up the zoo's gardens, a monkey named Razzle went missing. The zoo is closing, and police are looking for clues. Here is zoo director Sally Mander."

"We are so sad," the director said. "Our monkey is gone. And what's more, now our gardening won't get done. We have to send home all these nice people who are here to help."

"Ha!" Dad slapped his hands on the

steering wheel. "We got the monkey *and* we stopped their cleanup day!"

Mom turned around and scooped up the monkey in her arms. "What do you say, Razzle? Want to become a Crook like us?"

"Eh eeh!" Razzle screeched.

I felt horrible. I had gone to the zoo to help, but now because of my family, the zoo was in worse shape than before.

"Billy and Jillian, put on your glasses and wigs," Mom said. "You're going to pretend to be two grandmas taking the kid to the mall. We'll be right ahead of you, showing the fine art of picking pockets."

"Hot diggety!" Dad said, and hopped out.

"Go to Grandma," Mom said to Razzle.

Razzle grinned, leaped out of Mom's arms, and hopped right on my head.

6

Grandma Goes Bananas

"Watch us, Razzle," Mom said.
"Do what we do."

Mom and Dad started walking
toward the mall, acting like
construction workers on a break.
Dad glanced back.

Jillian got out, put Razzle in the
stroller, and tucked a blanket around
him. I put on my wig and started
pushing the stroller.

"This is a terrible idea," Jillian

said. "Mom and Dad don't know how to take care of a monkey."

"I know," I whispered back. "I always wanted a pet. But I was thinking more like a hamster."

We kept walking. Luckily, the stroller ride kept Razzle quiet.

"You know what I've been thinking?" Jillian whispered.

"What?"

She leaned toward me. "We are not a normal family."

Another case of major goose bumps! I'd been thinking the same thing.

She whispered, "When I was younger, I didn't know any better. I thought that every family was like ours. But lately I've been thinking we're strange. I think most moms and dads want their kids to be good."

"I've been wondering about that, too," I whispered back. "But I figured I was all alone. Ever since we moved here, you've been going out and stealing every day. Mom and Dad have been thrilled."

"I haven't been stealing," Jillian said.

"But you come home with something every day! A toaster, a watch, a bracelet . . ."

"I didn't steal any of those things. I snuck them out of the stash in our basement and acted as if they were new. We have so much stolen stuff, Mom and Dad can't even keep track of it."

I was shocked. "So where have you been going?"

"I've been going to the library, dressed like this. I've been helping older people learn how to use the computer. I've been doing good deeds."

I stopped pushing the stroller.

She smiled and shrugged. "It feels
great, Billy. I think Mom and Dad
might be wrong. I think doing
good might be good after all."

"We're both nuts!" I said.

"Actually, I think we're normal
and our parents are nuts," she said.
"But right now we've got a monkey
problem."

"Maybe Razzle will be a bad thief,"
I said. "Then Mom and Dad won't
want to keep him."

Mom looked back at us, so we
started walking again.

Just inside the front entrance of
the mall was a food court, and it was
jammed. Mom got in line at Salads
by Suzy, and Dad got in line at Pizza
Palace. We joined the line at Tootie

Frootie Smoothies, which was in between them.

"Oh, no," I whispered. "This is terrible."

"What?" Jillian whispered.

"There is no Beggin' fer Burgers in this mall!"

Jillian hit me with her purse.

Mom caught Razzle's attention by waving at him. I knew what was coming next. She was going to pick somebody's pocket.

Quickly, I crouched down by the stroller. "Do this, Razzle!" I stuck a finger up my nose.

A woman passing by looked at me like I was nuts.

Razzle kept his round eyes on Mom. She pulled a man's wallet out of his back pocket and slipped it into her own.

What Razzle did next was amazing. He reached into the pocket of the man standing in front of us and pulled out his wallet without even getting out of the stroller. Monkeys have long arms.

Then Razzle's
hairy hand
reached into
the purse of the
woman in front of
us. He slipped the
woman's wallet
right out of her
purse without
the woman even
feeling it.

Just our luck. We got ourselves a
pocket-picking genius.

Dad grinned. Mom motioned for
us to take Razzle back to the car.

Just then Razzle noticed all the
fruit on the counter of the Tootie
Frootie Smoothies booth. I always
thought cheetahs were the fastest

animals in the world, but this crazy little dude was faster. Before Jillian or I could blink, he ran to the booth, hopped up on the counter, grabbed a bunch of bananas, ran back, and jumped right into my arms.

"Hey!" the Tootie Frootie Smoothies guy yelled. "That baby stole my bananas!"

Everybody turned to look at me. Razzle buried his face in my shoulder, so all they could see was his bonnet and his pink onesie.

"What a horrible baby," a woman near me whispered.

"What a horrible grandmother," her friend whispered back. "I saw her trying to teach that baby how to pick her nose, too."

I looked at Jillian for help. She took a step away from me and said in her Mrs. Sippy voice, "I'd never let my grandchild steal fruit."

Thanks a lot, Jillian.

I walked over to the Tootie Frootie Smoothies guy, gave the bananas back, and headed out to the parking lot.

Jillian, Mom, and Dad joined me by the car a few minutes later. Mom and Dad were all smiles.

"Woohoo!" Dad said. "Razzle is a great Crook!"

"I love you, you crazy monkey!" Mom said, and gave the top of his baby bonnet a big kiss.

I looked down at Razzle. He smiled up at me, chocolate on his teeth and a candy bar wrapper in his hand.

"Hey!" I checked my purse. Sure enough, it was mine. "Gimme back my candy!" I said.

He stuck his finger in his mouth, wiped some chocolate off his teeth, and held it out for me to lick.

"Thanks, but no thanks," I said to the little monster. "I like my chocolate without the added flavor of monkey spit."

7

Try Our New
Ketchup Shampoo

Dinner. With a monkey. Not as fun as you'd think.

Here's what a monkey will do if you invite him over for dinner:

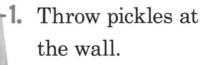 1. Throw pickles at the wall.

2. Sit his hairy 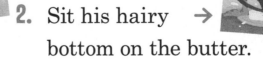 bottom on the butter.

3. Squeeze your cheeks together while you're trying to eat.
4. Stick French fries → in your socks.

5. Pour coffee on your hamburger.

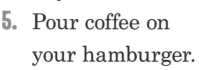

6. Shampoo your → sister's pigtails. With ketchup.

There was one thing that was good about dinner. It was nice to be back in jeans and a T-shirt. No wonder old ladies are sometimes crabby. Try wearing a dress and stockings all day, dude.

"Do you still think keeping the monkey is a good idea?" Jillian asked

Mom and Dad as she wiped the ketchup off her hair.

"He is a total nut-cup," I chimed in. "Maybe it's because he wants to be back with his family."

"Nonsense," Mom said. "He's happy here."

"I have a great idea," Dad said. "Let's take Curious George to the grocery store and steal some dessert."

"Love it!" Mom said. "Want to come, kids?"

"Well," Jillian said, "Billy should practice his lock picking."

"Hey!" I said. "Who made you boss?"

Jillian kicked me under the table.

I was about to say ouch when I realized that she had a plan. "Yeah. I guess I do need practice," I said.

"I'll stay home and make sure he does it right," Jillian said.

Mom and Dad smiled at each other proudly.

As soon as they were gone, Jillian started pacing. "We have to get that monkey back without Mom and Dad finding out. I think they've been spying on us, so we have to be extra careful."

"Why would they spy on us?"

"To make sure we're doing what they want us to do," she said. "To make sure that we're being crooks. If Mom and Dad catch on that we want to do good . . . well, I don't think they'd like it."

"So, what'll we do?"

"I think I have an idea," she said. "But I'm going to need your help." Jillian's pigtails looked like they'd been in a wrestling match, and she had ketchup on her forehead.

"I'm in," I said. "I just have one question."

"What's that?"

I pointed to her forehead. "Want some fries with that?"

8

Got Any Earwax?

"Helloooo!" Dad called out. "We have cookies and cake!"

Jillian and I had planned everything. "Remember, Billy," she said. "We need to act like we're tired and pretend to go to bed! Once you hear Mom and Dad go into their room, get ready."

As soon as we went into the kitchen, Razzle jumped off the kitchen table straight into my arms. If you think that sounds cute, that's because you've never had a stinking hair ball fly at your face. It's terrifying.

"We hit the bakery," Mom said. She set out chocolate cookies and a white frosted cake. In blue icing, on the top, it said

Some mothers probably bake cakes for their kids. My mother steals them. I wondered if the Grandpa Nelson on

the cake was the Mr. Nelson who lived
next door.

While Mom poured soda and Dad
opened the cookies, Razzle hopped
onto the counter and grabbed a bunch
of bananas. Then he jumped back into
my arms.

"E eeeh oo ee eeeh," he said,
sticking the bananas in my face.

"Fine," I said. "You can eat the
whole bunch."

He dangled the bananas in front
of my face again. "E eeeh oo ee eeeh."

He was trying to tell me
something. I plugged my nose to
block out his bad breath and looked
into his round eyes. He looked so
sad. I remembered the bananas on
the platform in the Monkey House.

I think he was saying, *I want to go home.*

"E eeeh oo ee eeeh?" I asked.

"E eeeh oo ee eeeh!" His round eyes flashed with excitement. He really was cute. Then the cute little guy bonked me on the head with the bananas.

"Cake or cookies, Billy?" Dad asked.

"It all looks yummy," I said.

Jillian elbowed me and yawned. "I'm too tired to eat, aren't you?" she said.

"Me? Too tired to eat?"

She elbowed me again.

Oh—the plan. "I'm too tired to eat, too." I yawned.

Razzle yawned.

Good Razzle!

"Razzle looks tired, too," Jillian said. "Didn't you make a bed for him in your room?"

"Yes, I did," I said. "I'll take him up."

"Oooh eeeah," the monkey said.

"Good night, kids," Mom and Dad said. "Good night, monkey."

Jillian, Razzle, and I ran upstairs. I took Razzle into my room, and Jillian went into hers.

I set him down in the bed I made out of a laundry basket. "Don't worry, Razzle. We're going to take you back soon. Just pretend to sleep. Nighty night, Razzle. Go to sleepy!" To show him what I meant, I closed my eyes and snored.

Razzle flopped down on his bed and started to snore, too.

I'm telling you, dude, if this monkey went to Hollywood, he'd land a starring role right away.

I crawled into my bed and turned out the light.

All part of the plan.

I waited until I heard the door to Mom and Dad's bedroom close.

"Come on, Razzle. We have to make it look like we're here sleeping." I put a pile of dirty clothes under my covers to look like my body. Next, I put a wig stuffed with a toilet-paper roll facedown on the pillow for my head. I created a fake body in Razzle's bed and put a toilet-paper roll inside his baby bonnet for his head.

Next, I tucked my cell phone under my pillow, so if my parents were tracking my phone, they'd think I was still in bed. Brilliant idea. Not mine. Yep, you guessed it. Jillian's idea.

"Come on, Razzle," I whispered.

He hopped onto my back and stuck his fingers in my ears. I tiptoed into

Jillian's room, not making a sound. At least I didn't hear myself making any sounds.

"Wome on, Wiwwy," Jillian whispered. "Wet's wake wis wonkey wo whe woo."

"I can't hear you," I said.

She pulled the monkey's fingers out of my ears and repeated her sentence: "Come on, Billy. Let's take this monkey to the zoo."

"Wow," I whispered. "I heard that loud and clear. Thanks, Razzle."

"What are you thanking him for?" Jillian asked.

"I think he got all of the wax out of my ears," I said.

Razzle smiled and then licked his fingers.

You know what they say: one man's earwax is another man's frosting.

9

Oops. Wrong Way.

 Imagine the picture. A clear black sky lit by a bright white moon. I was following Jillian, riding my bike with Razzle on my back. The road was under my tires, the feel of the wind was in my hair, and monkey claws were digging into my shoulders.

It was eleven o'clock that Saturday night. We were pedaling like crazy.

"Ooo! Ooo!" Razzle kept screeching.

I swear that hairy little guy knew we were headed to the zoo.

We passed by a Beggin' fer Burgers. The smell of bacon burgers filled the night air and went up my nostrils. "Jillian, let's stop—"

"No way." My sister kept pedaling. "We don't have time."

"Next time you want to invent something," I called out to her, "invent me a sister who likes bacon burgers as much as me."

She did not reply.

When we got to the zoo, Jillian used the Popper to unlock

the back gate. We left our bikes by a Dumpster and headed toward the Monkey House. The moonlight cast eerie shadows, making the trees and buildings look creepy. We tiptoed past the Small Mammal House, the Reptile House, and a large grassy picnic area badly in need of mowing.

The zoo really did need some gardening help!

As we passed by a low brick wall, Razzle jumped onto my head and started screeching.

To my right, a huge RRROOOOOAAAARRRR split the air. The Lions' Den!

Razzle jumped onto Jillian's head, and she and I took off running.

We were out of breath by the time

we got to the Monkey House.

Razzle was beyond excited. He leaped onto the bars of the house. In the dim light, we could see the other monkeys coming to greet him.

"Eehhe!" Razzle's sister, Dazzle, jumped up and down on the platform, waving her arms.

"Now, that's a sister who appreciates her bro," I said.

Razzle jumped onto Jillian's shoulder and grabbed the Popper. Before Jillian could stop him, he pointed it at the cage door. *CLICK!*
NO!

All the monkeys rushed out to welcome him! Dazzle was first and she gave Razzle a big hug.

"Get back in!" Jillian shouted.

Razzle and Dazzle held hands and jumped up and down.

I tried to chase the monkeys back in the cage while Jillian tried to get the Popper out of Razzle's hand. But Razzle pushed the button again.

"OH, NO!" Jillian screamed.

The Popper was pointed at the gate to the Giraffe Village.

A beautiful slender giraffe trotted out, followed by another and another and another. They started nibbling on the leaves of the trees.

"Razzle!" Jillian exclaimed. "Give that back right now."

Razzle turned to the left and pushed the button again. Out leaped the gazelles. They took off for the meadow. Grinning, he faced the Elephant Yard.

"Yo, monkey boy!" I said. "Stop messing with the hardware. Now, give it up." I held out my hand.

Razzle looked at me, his teeth flashing in the moonlight. Then he pushed the button.

The heavy metal gate groaned as it opened. An elephant stomped out and stopped to go to the bathroom right in the middle of the sidewalk.

I guess elephants don't need privacy.

"Billy," Jillian yelled, "shut the gate before—"

Too late—a whole crowd of elephants ran out.

A stampede!

The monkeys scampered up into the trees.

"Run!" Jillian yelled.

The elephants were running straight at us.

What happened next felt as if it happened in slow motion. Jillian and I ran, the pounding of huge elephant feet in our ears, the smell of elephant you-know-what in our nostrils. We ran for our lives. And when you are running for your life, you are not always thinking clearly. We ran . . .

Right into the monkeys' cage.

You can probably guess what happened next.

Yep.

Razzle smiled and locked us in.

10

Would You Like to Swing on a Tire?

From inside the locked Monkey House, we watched more elephants march out of the Elephant Yard. Several of them stopped to leave a souvenir along the way.

"Droppings" is a polite way to describe the doo-doo that elephants will do-do on the sidewalk if you let them. Another word is elephant "pie."

But I have to tell you, when it comes
to elephants, a "dropping" or a "pie" is
more like a GIANT STINK BOMB.
We could smell it in the Monkey
House even with our noses plugged.

But that, of course, wasn't the real
problem. The real problem was that I
still had wax in my ears. Just kidding.
The real problem was that the snack
bar was closed. Just kidding. Sort of.
Actually, the real problem was that we
had more than one problem.

Problems:
1. We were locked in the Monkey
   House.
2. Monkeys, giraffes, gazelles, and
   elephants were running wild.
3. My stomach was growling.

"A Tootie Frootie Smoothie would taste good right now," I said.

"Focus, Billy," Jillian said.

"Well," I said, "we are lucky about a few things."

"Like what?"

"Like, at least Razzle didn't let out the lions and tigers and bears."

"Not yet!" she said. "We have to get the Popper back before he does!"

I climbed onto a platform.

"Are you climbing up to get a better view of the zoo?" Jillian asked.

"No. I'm climbing up to play on the tire swing," I said. "If you get locked in the Monkey House, you might as well have a little fun, Jillian. That's how I roll."

"Have a little fun?" My sister

gave me one of her looks.

"Yeah. You know, have fun, get your swing on, go ape."

"This is serious," Jillian said. "Razzle!" she called out. "Get over here and hand me that Popper!"

I jumped onto the tire swing and went sailing across the cage.

"Billy! That's not helping."

"Yelling at the monkeys isn't helping, either," I said.

Jillian plopped down on a bale of hay and stared at her feet. "This is a disaster."

I swung higher. "Ee eh eh!" I screeched, and laughed.

"This isn't playtime!" Jillian said.

I locked my legs around the tire, let go of the rope, and hung upside

down. "Wooooooo-eeeeeeee!"

My sister's upside-down face looked as red as a burning stick of dynamite. "Get down from there, Billy."

The monkeys were looking in at me. "Eh ee eee eee!" I waved.

Razzle and Dazzle waved back. Razzle climbed over to get a better look.

When the tire swing reached the

platform, I hopped off. I grabbed a banana. "Ee eh eh!"

"I get it," Jillian whispered. "Monkey see, monkey do. You're making them want to come back in!"

Actually, I was getting a banana because I was hungry. But making the monkeys want back in was a good idea.

I stuffed the banana into my mouth and rubbed my tummy. Then I dangled another banana in front of Razzle. While Razzle reached in, I reached out, slipping my fingers between the bars. Quickly, I grabbed ahold of the Popper and slipped it back through.

Score!

"Go, Billy!" Jillian clapped.

I looked at the monkeys. "Dudes, you have to come inside to get bananas!" Pointing the Popper at the door, I pushed the button and the lock popped open.

Razzle and the other monkeys rushed in. Jillian and I ran out, locking the door behind us.

"Billy!" Jillian started dancing. "You're a genius!"

"Thank you! Thank you!" I bowed to my imaginary audience. Then I stepped in a steaming hot jumbo elephant pie.

11

What Is Cute and Gray and Wrinkled? Me.

"We have to split up," Jillian said. "We have to get the animals back in their pens before they figure out a way to leave the zoo. I'll do the gazelles and giraffes. You do the elephants."

"Thanks a lot!"

"I'm doing two," she argued.

I plugged my nose. "But the one

I'm doing makes doo-doo pies the size of Montana."

"That gives me a great idea!" she exclaimed. "I'm going to use a smell to herd the animals back in."

"A good smell?" I asked. "Like bacon?"

"No." She rolled her eyes. "I'll get something that smells like a lion and use it to chase the gazelles and giraffes into their pens."

"What should I do?"

She shrugged. "Figure something out, Billy." Off she ran.

How would *you* get twelve elephants back into the Elephant Yard?

I took off in the direction the elephants had gone. *The zoo is a big place,* I thought. *How am I going to be able to find them?* And then I went *squish!*

Another elephant pie fresh out of the oven, if you know what I mean. Well, I was on the right track. I followed the stinky pies past Great Meadow Trail and down Sea Lion Lane to Birdhouse Walk.

Twelve dark, hunky shapes were standing near the fountain in front of the Birdhouse. A couple of them were drinking out of the fountain.

"Hey," I said. "Any chance you'd all like to go back home now?"

A couple of birds tweeted. Nothing from the elephants.

I tried Plan B. "Ladies and gentlemen! Free popcorn in the Elephant Yard."

Not a word.

"Gosh, dudes. You could at least answer," I said. An elephant at the fountain lifted her trunk and sprayed me.

"Thanks," I said. "I needed a shower."

It was better than ketchup.

Moving on to Plan C. Since Monkey See, Monkey Do had worked, then maybe Elephant See, Elephant Do would work. I found two big paper bags in a trash can. I tore elephant ear shapes out of one and twisted strips of the other to form a trunk and a tail. I tore slits in the ears and stuck them onto my own ears. Then I tucked the tail into the back of my pants and held the trunk on my nose.

Slowly, I walked to the front,

swaying my trunk. The elephants
checked me out. I began to sing a
little song.

(To the tune of "My Darling Clementine")
"I'm a darling, I'm a darling,
   I'm a darling elephant.
I'm so charming, gray, and
      wrinkled.
I just tinkled in my pants!"

I looked back. The elephants were
staring at me.

"Follow me-o, Mama me-o, back to
      our big stinky yard.
We will dance like Queens of
      France,
And then we'll play a game of cards!"

I felt a tug. An elephant had grabbed my tail! She wanted to follow me! I kept singing and walking. Another elephant grabbed her tail. And another and another. It was working!

"To the right-o, to the left-o, let us swing our trunks so high.
Shake our booties, 'cause we're cuties.
Then we'll sing our lullaby."

I led the parade into the Elephant Yard.

"Oh my gnarly, oh my gnarly, oh my gnarly chunky chums.
Time for beddie, rest our headies And our great big hunky bums!"

All the elephants went in. They actually sat down, resting their great big hunky bums. I ran out and locked the gate. Perhaps there was a career for me in elephant herding. If so, I'd need to buy one thing: a good pair of nose plugs.

I turned around to look for Jillian, and that's when I saw it. Her torn jacket was on the

sidewalk in front of the Gazelle Pen. I ran over and picked it up. Whew! Smelled like a cat.

Uh-oh, I thought. *The only kind of cats in here are big ones.* What if Jillian had used a lion to scare the gazelles and giraffes back into their yards and then the lion had used *her* for a midnight snack? Her hair

probably still smelled like ketchup,
which would have attracted the lion to
her even more.

"JILLIAN?" I screamed.

12

Lion Meat

Let me tell you, when you're standing all alone in a dark zoo and you think a lion has eaten your twin sister, you really start to miss her.

"Jillian?" I called out. "Are you okay?"

No answer.

When your poor sister doesn't answer, you start to picture her in your mind. You think about her skinny arms and knobby knees. You realize that she wouldn't make for a very big snack. She has big ears, but how filling can an ear be? You stop thinking about your poor sister and start thinking about the poor lion, who is probably still hungry. Then you get scared.

"Lion?" I called, my own knobby knees shaking. "If you're out there, I want you to know that I am much skinnier than my sister."

No answer.

A cloud slid its dark hand over the moon and the night grew blacker. I shivered.

From behind me came a low growl: "Grrrr."

Too terrified to turn around, I took one baby step away. "Please don't eat me!"

"GRRRRR!"

"My arms taste like stale cheese doodles," I added, taking one more step. "And my legs taste like old celery."

"GRRRRRRRRRRRRR!"

Just as I was about to take off running, claws dug into my shoulders. I screamed! The claws spun me around and I came face to face with . . . Jillian.

She laughed. "I really got you, Billy!"

I almost wet my pants.

"Very funny," I said. "And to think I was sad that you might have been lion meat."

"Aw, my bro loves me!" She punched me on the arm.

"I'm going to get you back when you least expect it, Sis! Hey, by the way, what happened to this?" I held out her jacket.

She grinned. "All part of my plan. I found a clump of lion hair on the bushes by the Lions' Den and rubbed it all over my jacket. Then I used it to herd the gazelles and giraffes back. Smart, huh?"

Yep. Here's how Jillian got her animals back in:

And here's how I got my animals back in:

THE **SILLY** METHOD

b) FOLLOWERS

a) LEADER

"Come on, Billy. We have to cover our tracks and scram," Jillian said.

Covering our tracks meant getting rid of evidence. Usually that meant wiping fingerprints off doorknobs, but in this case it meant cleaning up GIANT STINK BOMBS. We didn't want anybody to know that the animals had been out of their pens, so we had to make the zoo look normal.

We found a couple of shovels in a shed by the Elephant Yard and shoveled all the elephant pies into the flower beds along Great Meadow Trail and then covered that with straw. Afterward, we hosed down the sidewalk.

Finally, we stopped by the Monkey House to say good-bye. Razzle was stuffing his face with bananas.

The clouds had split, and moonlight was shining on us like a spotlight. The sidewalk was sparkling. After all we had been through, I didn't feel like an ordinary good-bye was enough. This called for a speech.

I hopped up on a bench and held out my arms to the monkeys. "Farewell, monkeys, one and all! And most especially to you, Razzle." I put one hand over my heart. "I hereby forgive you for all the nasty things you did to me—"

"And me!" Jillian added.

"Yep. We forgive the fingers up our noses and the ketchup on our heads. We're sure you are a very nice monkey who was upset because our parents kidnapped you. So may you live long and—"

"Eh eeee," Razzle screeched, and

threw a banana peel in my face.

"Okay. Now, that was just plain rude!"

Jillian tugged my shirt. "Come on, we have to get out of here!"

"But—"

"Come on, Billy."

She pulled me off the bench.

"See you later, chump!" I said to Razzle.

He laughed.

13

Cakewalk

*W*hew. Who knew monkeys were so much work?

We got our bikes and rode home. We were hoping the wind would carry the smell off our clothes. But by the time we pulled into our driveway, we still stank.

We snuck into the house, peeked in on Mom and Dad to make sure they were still asleep, removed the pillows and toilet-paper rolls from our beds, and changed into fresh clothes. Jillian opened my window to make it look as if Razzle had escaped. And then we tiptoed down to the kitchen. We were hungry and wanted a snack before going back to bed.

I pulled out the cake. *Get Well, Grandpa Nelson.* Yum. Nobody had sliced into it yet. I got a knife and . . .

I just couldn't do it. I kept thinking about old Mr. Nelson next door and how he might be sick.

"Let's make a delivery," I said, and she nodded.

We ran out and put the cake on a little table on his front porch. We were about to leave when Jillian noticed weeds growing in his flower bed. She looked at me with a smile. *Yank! Yoink! Yank!* Take that!

Two good deeds in one from Billy and Jillian Crook. Yep. That's how we roll.

When we got home, we found peanut butter and spread it on . . . what else? Bananas!

"Even though he was a pain, I'm going to miss Razzle," Jillian said.

To cheer her up, I hopped on my chair and started making monkey faces. She laughed so hard, she knocked over the jar of peanut butter.

We heard a sound upstairs.

"They're up!" Jillian whispered. "Act normal!"

"How?" I whispered back. "I don't know what to say!"

"Just eat!" She shoved a banana in my face.

In the middle of a bite, Mom and Dad walked in.

"What are you two doing here?" Mom asked. "We heard noises."

"We were hungry," Jillian said.

"Where's Razzle?" Dad said, looking around. "He isn't down here?"

"Mmm mn," I mumbled, still with a full mouth.

"We checked your room. You left your window open, Billy." My mom looked at me like I had monkey brains. "He must have escaped."

I swallowed. "Really?"

"Actually, that hairy dude was a pain," Dad said. "Tomorrow I think we should come up with a new crime to commit. Come on, Tanya. Let's go back to sleep."

They headed down the hall. *Whew!*

Jillian leaned in and whispered. "Good job."

"Thanks," I whispered back.

"Just do one more thing," she said.

"What?"

"Give yourself a shampoo," she said. "You still smell like a zoo."

14

Happily Elephant After

"**G**rrrrr."

I woke up the next morning to a terrifying sound.

"GRRRRRRRR!"

I clutched my blanket tighter. Oh, no! Had my parents stolen a lion? Or was Jillian playing another trick on me by acting like a lion?

I looked around. The sun was streaming through my window. No lion. No Jillian.

"GRRRRRRRRRRRRRRR!"

I looked down. It was my stomach rumbling.

Time for breakfast.

As I passed Jillian's room, I peeked in. She was still sleeping. Very unusual. But then again, herding wild animals and cleaning up after them is pretty unusual, too. I went downstairs and opened the fridge. A jar of hot fudge sauce. A six-pack of soda.

Ketchup. A plate of cold French fries.

None of it sounded good. I had a craving for . . . bacon, scrambled eggs, and toast. Maybe a glass of orange juice and a slice of melon to go with it. A normal breakfast? What was next?

I found some bread in the freezer and made toast. While I was eating, I opened up the laptop that was on the table and searched the headlines for the top news videos.

"NEW PRESIDENT PAINTS WHITE HOUSE GREEN"

"KITTENS FOUND ON MARS"

"THIRD GRADER WINS MILLION-DOLLAR LOTTERY"

Why isn't the news ever interesting?
I thought. And then I
saw it:

"MONKEY RETURNED TO ZOO"

I clicked on the video.

A reporter was standing in front
of the Elephant Yard. "I'm Saya Lott,
and I'm here at the zoo with a news
update: a happy ending for Razzle the
monkey. Last night, the zoo seems to
have been visited by some mysterious
do-gooders."

I got Jillian.

"You have to see this," I
whispered. We tiptoed back to the
kitchen and watched the video.

"Not only did the mysterious

do-gooders return Razzle, but they also mowed the grass, trimmed the trees, and fertilized the garden with elephant droppings. The zoo looks great. Here to tell us more about it is zoo director Sally Mander."

The camera focused on the director. "We're delighted! Razzle is back and doing fine. And the zoo is looking better than ever! It's as if a herd of volunteers came through the zoo overnight."

"Wow," Jillian said. "The gazelles must have eaten the grass, and the giraffes must have trimmed the trees when they were out of their pens."

"Yeah," I said. "And when we shoveled all the elephant droppings into the bushes, I had no idea we were fertilizing the garden!"

We turned back to the news clip.

Sally Mander was showing off the rosebushes. "What a great idea to use elephant droppings as garden fertilizer! We can raise money for the zoo by selling it. A truckload of elephant droppings for only twenty-five dollars. We'll never run out of it!"

"You heard it, folks," Saya Lott said. "Support the zoo by buying elephant droppings for your garden. Any last words, Ms. Mander?"

The zoo director took the microphone and looked directly into the camera. "We want to say two words to whoever came here last night: Thank you! And to all of you out there listening, just remember:

you will always succeed if you do a good deed."

Jillian and I started dancing around the kitchen.

"I feel great," Jillian said.

"Me, too," I said.

Jillian smiled. "I have a feeling

this is just the beginning. I bet we can do more secret good deeds."

More good deeds. More adventures. More bacon along the way.

That's how I roll.

Secret Extras

SECRET FACT

Many zoos do sell elephant droppings to gardeners. Louisville, Kentucky, raised money for its zoo from the sale of Zoo Poopy Doo, which is hay, straw, and wood shavings mixed with elephant droppings. Now, that's clever recycling!

Do not—we repeat, do not—try this at home. We're sure your elephant prefers using the toilet. Just kidding.

Your elephant probably never poops. Just kidding. You probably don't even have an elephant. Yet.

SECRET RIDDLE

What do you call a monkey and an elephant in the North Pole?*

*Very lost

SECRET GAME
The Elephant Parade

This is straight-up fun and you will *not* need any elephant poop to play this game. All you need are two old paper bags.

1. With the help of a grown-up, cut two long strips out of one paper bag.

2. Twist one strip to form a tail.

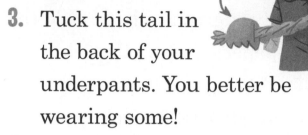

3. Tuck this tail in the back of your underpants. You better be wearing some!

4. Twist the other strip of the paper bag into a trunk. Set this aside.

5. With a grown-up's help, cut big elephant ears out of the other paper bag.

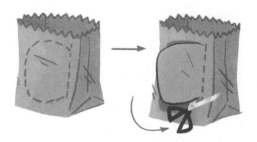

6. Tear slits in the paper ears.

7. Put the paper ears on your own, sticking your own ears through the slits to hold the paper ears in place.
8. Pick up the trunk and hold it on your nose.
9. Walk around in a single file line, swinging your trunk and singing the song on page 121.

Make sure to do this in front of grown-ups. If they say, "Why are you acting like nuts?" say, "We're not nuts—we're elephants, thank you very much!"

The Elephant Parade Song
(To the tune of "My Darling Clementine")

I'm a darl ing, I'm a darling, I'm a darl ing el e phant.
Follow me- o, Ma ma me- o, back to our big stin ky yard.
To the right- o, to the left- o, let us swing our trunks so high.
Oh my gnar ly, oh my gnar ly, oh my gnar ly chun ky chums.

I'm so charm ing, gray and wrin kled. I just tin kled in my pants!
We will dance like Queens of France, and then we'll play a game of cards!
Shake our boo ties, 'cause we're cu ties. Then we'll sing our lull a by.
Time for bed die, rest our head ies, and our great big hun ky bums!

121